THE Christmas of the Reddle Moon

BY J. Patrick Lewis • PICTURES BY Gary Kelley

 DIAL BOOKS NEW YORK

For Marty
J. P. L.

For my mother
G. K.

———————————

Published by Dial Books
A Division of Penguin Books USA Inc.
375 Hudson Street, New York, New York 10014

Text copyright © 1994 by J. Patrick Lewis
Pictures copyright © 1994 by Gary Kelley
All rights reserved / Designed by Atha Tehon
Printed in Hong Kong
First Edition
1 3 5 7 9 10 8 6 4 2

Library of Congress Cataloging in Publication Data
Lewis, J. Patrick.
The Christmas of the reddle moon / by J. Patrick Lewis ;
pictures by Gary Kelley.—1st ed.
p. cm.
Summary: Lost in a snowstorm on an English heath on Christmas Eve,
Liddy and Will meet the magical and mysterious Wee Mary Fever,
who summons St. Nick himself to take them home.
ISBN 0-8037-1566-8 (trade).—ISBN 0-8037-1567-6 (library)
[1. Christmas—Fiction. 2. Magic—Fiction. 3. Santa Claus—Fiction.
4. England—Fiction.] I. Kelley, Gary, ill. II. Title.
PZ7.L5866Ch 1994 [E]—dc20 93-28049 CIP AC

*The full-color artwork was prepared with pastels on paper.
It was then color-separated and reproduced in
red, yellow, blue, and black halftones.*

A U T H O R ' S   N O T E

The heath in this story refers to a vast expanse of meadow or moorland once common in rural England. Strewn with pebbles and moss and wildflowers in spring, it was a delight to the eye; but in winter, especially at night, the heath was a forbidding and mysterious place to be.

Reddle is the name of a red clay, dug from the ground, and sold to sheep farmers, who used it for marking sheep. This is a long forgotten form of branding. Reddle-sellers like Wee Mary Fever were mysterious too. Proud of their independence, they traveled the heath alone, and were either feared or scorned for their solitary way of life and the oddity of their trade. As Thomas Hardy put it in *The Return of the Native*, mothers used to warn misbehaving children, "'The reddleman is coming for you!'"

The last reddle-seller died around 1920.

Once long ago, on the coldest Christmas Eve ever, a thick quilt of snow covered the dark heaths of England, and the promise of more hung in the ragged-tooth sky. Inside a stone cottage Liddy and Will Yeobright had bundled up for a winter walk to visit their cousins who lived on Thimble Hill.

"Please, Mother," Will asked, "may we stay for supper at Aunt Nora's?"

"Only for a cup of tea, Will. A blizzard's coming, I can feel it in my bones," said Mrs. Yeobright. "And besides, children must be home and long to bed if they expect a visit from Father Christmas!"

"Then hurry, Will!" said Liddy. "We haven't much time!"

So out the door they ran, down to the humpbacked bridge, around the curve of Puddletown Road. And it wasn't long before they saw the smoke rising from Aunt Nora's chimney.

Warmed by the fire, they ate plum pudding, drank hot tea, and listened too long to stories of Christmases past. For when the clock chimed six, Liddy remembered her mother's warning. She and Will exchanged the sacks of presents with their cousins, kissed Aunt Nora good-bye, and started for home.

But darkness had fallen fast, not a sliver of moon lit the land. The wind wolf-howled. "This way, Will!" said Liddy, trying her best to be brave. "There's a shortcut over the heath."

"My bag's so heavy I can't carry it!" grumbled Will, following after her.

They were trudging along, tramping through knee-high drifts, when a violent snowstorm came bucketing out of the sky.

"Help, Liddy, help! I can't see!"

"Here, take my hand!"

But it was hopelessly dark, sleet swirled all around. And there on the wild heath Liddy and Will Yeobright huddled together, cold and lost, not knowing which way to go.

Then, as if out of nowhere, there appeared a strange red ball of light!

"Just a little farther, Will! I think there's someone to help us." Liddy pulled him along down a steep slope.

All of a sudden the snow gave way! Will fell first and Liddy tumbled on top of him into a deep pit as Aunt Nora's presents split open and flew everywhere!

Liddy tried to shout, to scream for help, but her voice was lost in the storm. The last thing she saw as she looked up to the pit's black rim were the diamond eyes of an enormous cat.

Now in those days an old woman—Wee Mary Fever was her name—lived all alone on the heath in her caravan, two shaggy ponies and a cat the color of fire her only company. Day after day she dug in the pits for reddle, a kind of clay named for its bright color, which she sold to sheep farmers who used it to mark their sheep.

It was said in the long-tongued towns that she had a heart of iron and a bloodred face as wrinkled as the sea. Stories about the old woman grew into legend. Each year the legend grew until it was nothing but half-truths. And no telling which half the truth might be.

But this much was certain. The ball of light that Liddy had seen belonged to Wee Mary Fever.

And the diamond eyes were the eyes of her fire-cat.

And this was the bottom of her very own pit.

Liddy and Will awoke in a strange place. Their presents sat nearby, wrapped as neatly as if Aunt Nora had done it herself. Inside the covered van an old woman was knitting a beautiful stocking, which was as red as the rest of her. She held up the pair, and by the light of a coal lantern admired her work.

"Excuse me," Liddy whispered.

Wee Mary Fever turned quickly. "You took a fair knock in the pit," she said in a voice dry as dust. "Lucky for you Old Diggory was out to prowl." Beside her the huge red cat licked its paw.

Winter shook the curtains. "It's no night for travelers," she added, and passed them half a loaf of miller's bread and a tin full of hot broth to share.

"Do you know what I be, my little pigeons?"

"The reddlewoman?" Liddy replied fearfully.

"Aye! You're as skittery as spring lambs! Afraid of a wee woman as red as turnips?"

Now faster than wild deer the gossip ran, and some said that Mary Fever kept a secret bowlful of reddle, cinnamon, dillweed, and the bones of snowy owls and whoever else happened by. No one had ever seen the reddlewoman's dust, but that didn't stop them from guessing its hidden powers.

Will had heard the gossip too. "You won't be crushing our bones to powder, will you, Mum?"

"Hush, Will!" said Liddy.

The old woman shook her head. "Half of what you hear about the reddlepeople is bunk, the other half is rubbish."

"But how will we get home from here?" said Will, holding back tears. "This is Christmas Eve! We're sure to miss St. Nicholas!"

Even as Will spoke, the reddlewoman was drawing her fingers gently over their eyes, and the children fell fast asleep.

Then, quickly, she took out her porcelain bowl and set to work, mixing this and that and who could guess what else. All the while she sang softly to the cat:

A pinch of fire,
A nip of night,
A twist of fate,
My diamond-bright.
Two cups of clay,
Three tablespoons
Of mist will make
My reddle moon!

The ponies whinnied, Old Diggory leaped over the lantern
—a sure sign that someone was coming! But this the
reddlewoman already knew. For she scooped a handful of
grounds from her bowl, opened the window, and blew them
into the night.

Whooosh! A flash!

And there it was again! Red circle of light! Just like the one
that Liddy and Will had seen before.

High above the heath, St. Nick drove his reindeer through
the cloud-bank. Many were his stops before morning, but the
mysterious light below beckoned to him. So he pulled on the
reins and glided his sleigh down for a closer look.

Just as he was landing, the red moon grew pink and pale,
then vanished altogether. Blackest night returned.

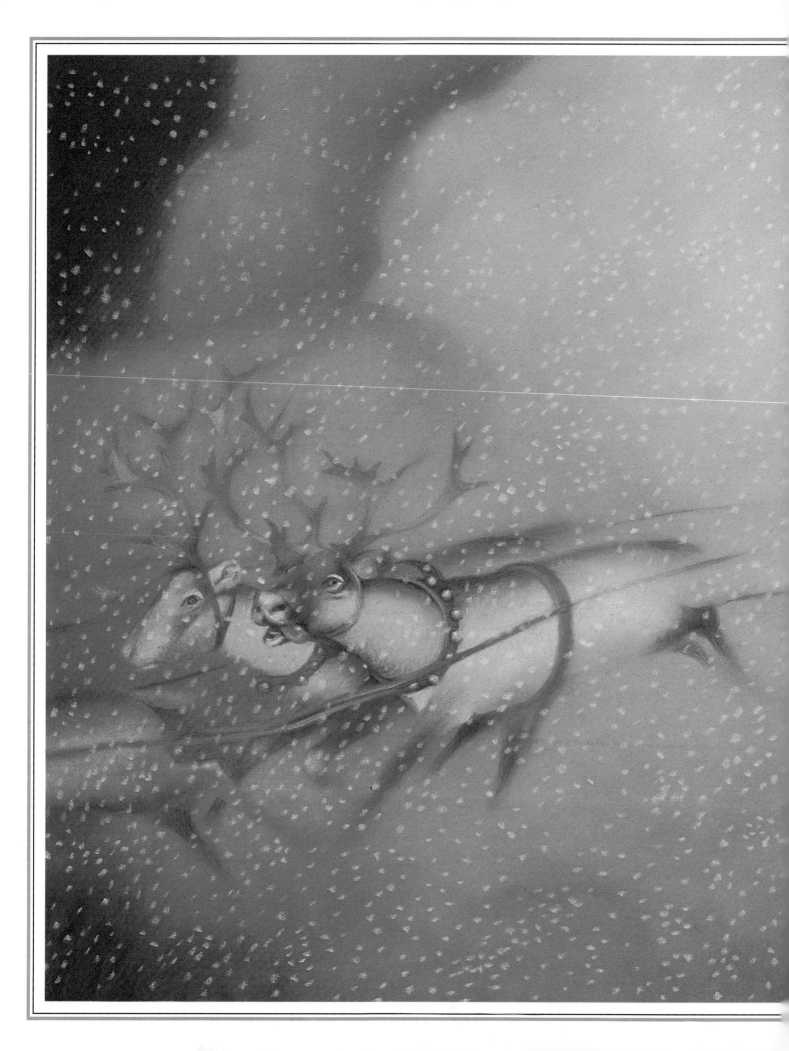

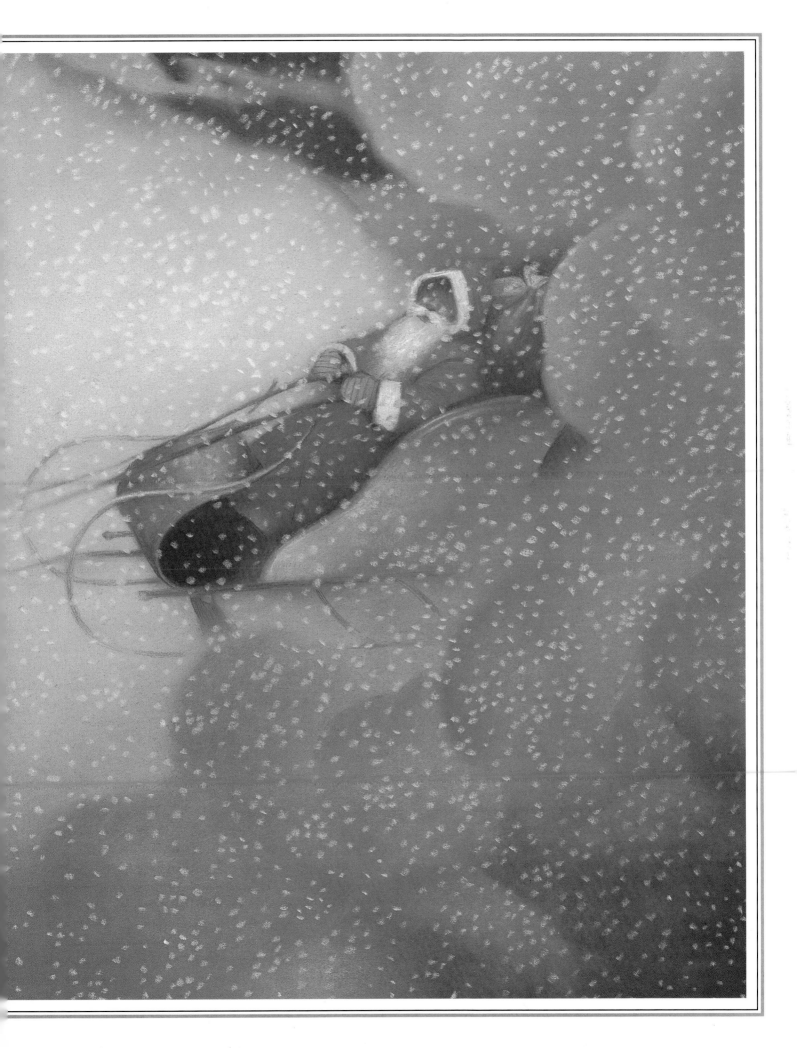

The old woman held out her lantern as St. Nicholas climbed into the van.

"Welcome, traveler!" She bowed slightly and handed him a cup of broth. "I'm Wee Mary Fever. Say hello to Old Diggory."

"A scarlet cat! Red walls? And you…!" he exclaimed, but he was too polite to say more. Except for the whites of her eyes and her teeth, he could see that she was perfectly, brilliantly red from head to toe.

They talked about hard winters and spring floods, good cats and good company, stray lambs and flying reindeer—any subject but the one staring him in the face.

"My dear woman," he said at last, "you lit this Christmas Eve with a red moon, then you made it disappear!"

"A *reddle* moon, sir!" she corrected him, her eyes shining like stars. "And isn't this the one time of year for a pinch of magic?"

St. Nicholas laughed out loud. "Indeed it is, Mrs. Fever! Now will you please tell me what I can do to repay your kindness?"

"The favor of getting two lost children safely home…" she said. And she added with a mischievous smile, "…before St. Nicholas comes!"

Quietly he pulled back the bed curtain.

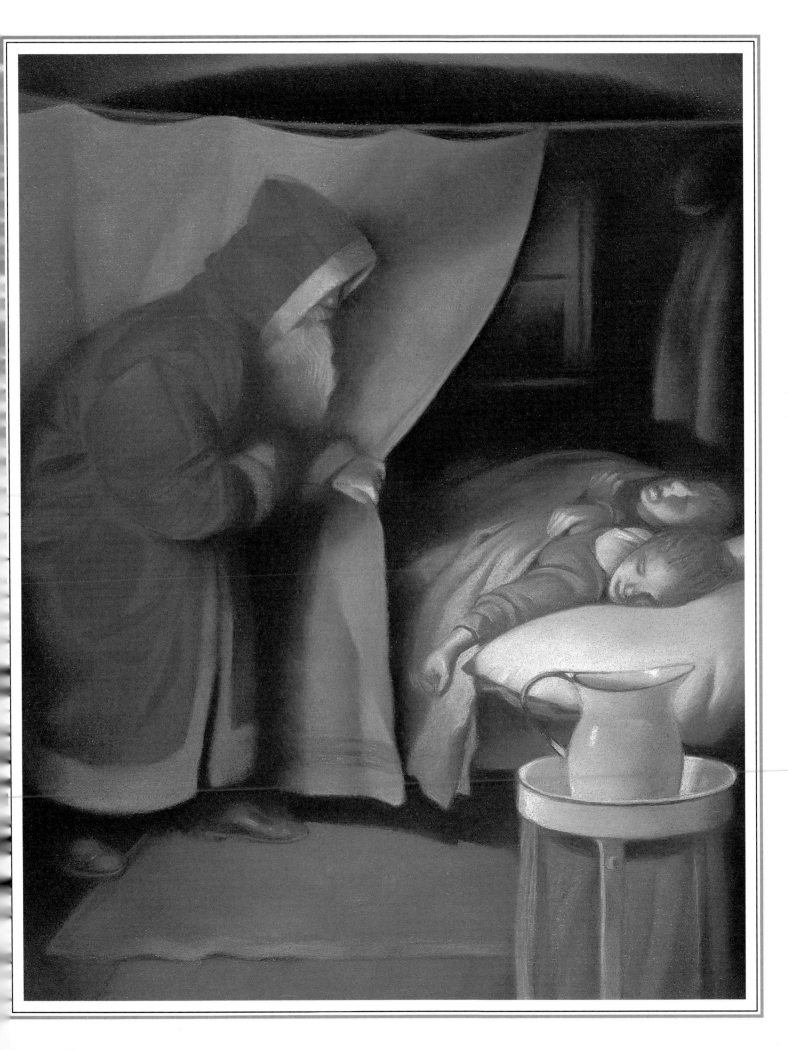

"Why, it's young Will and his sister Liddy from Puddletown! This far from home on Christmas Eve? Mr. and Mrs. Yeobright must be looking everywhere!"

"Wait," said Mary Fever. Hastily she wrapped something in a small packet, handed it to him, and whispered a secret in his ear. St. Nick stuffed the package into his pocket and stepped out into the storm. He lifted the children, still sleeping, into the sleigh, took the reins, and looked back.

"A Merry Christmas to you, Mary Fever—and to Old Diggory too!"

As the reindeer leaped from the frozen heath, she shouted after him, "Next year...watch for the moon! The reddle—!" But St. Nick was already flying toward the stars.

Fearing their children were lost, Mr. and Mrs. Yeobright had braved the cold to look for them. No one was home when the sleigh touched down in the snow-covered garden.

St. Nick carried Liddy and Will into the cottage, laid them gently in their beds, then set the presents out under the tree. Just before he left, he took Wee Mary Fever's package from his pocket. Off came the string and paper. And there on the mantel over the fireplace, he kept his promise to the reddlewoman.

Later that night the Yeobrights returned, overcome with happiness to find their children safe in their beds.

"Where on earth could they have gone?" asked Mrs. Yeobright.

But Mr. Yeobright was too tired to wake them, so he and his wife went off to bed.

When Liddy and Will awoke on Christmas Day, they told what they could remember of a night on the heath. Ice storms, dark pits, diamond eyes. And in the story everything was red— the moon, the cat, and the kind old woman. But neither of the children knew how they had found their way back to the cottage.

"Liddy," said Mr. Yeobright, "the heath can play tricks on a child's mind. You've had a nightmare. Nothing more."

"But look, Father!" cried Will, shaking the boxes under the tree. "We made it home in time for St. Nick!"

Indeed they had. Dry logs crackled in the hearth and when
Liddy looked up, she knew it wasn't a dream at all.

For there over the fireplace hung the gift of the reddlewoman—
the beautiful pair of knitted red stockings.

Not long after the first Christmas of the reddle moon, Wee Mary Fever died. She was the last of the reddlepeople. The story of Liddy and Will's adventure ran quickly down the long-tongued towns. But this time another legend grew—one that changed forever the way the old woman would be remembered.

On Christmas Eve, so the villagers say, when snow cancels out the sky and horses whisper steam in their stalls and the wind has stopped to catch its breath, peek through your curtain....

If you can see, even for an instant, a red ball of light beaming in the cold sky, St. Nicholas cannot be far away.